Strawberry Shortcake CRAFTS CLUB

BERRY BEST FRIENDS BOOK

A Fun with Friends Adventure

by Alison Saeger Panik

Scholastic Inc.

New York   Toronto   London   Auckland   Sydney   Mexico City   New Delhi   Hong Kong   Buenos Aires

ISBN: 0-439-70469-3

Designer: Emily Muschinske
Illustrations: Lisa and Terry Workman
Photographs: Alison Saeger Panik
Corinne Walker and Julia Becchinelli are pictured in the photos on page 11.
Jennifer Smalls, Chloe Argento, Gabe Houser and Grace Houser are pictured in the photos on page 17.

12 11 10 9 8 7 6 5 4 3 2 1   5 6 7 8 9 10/0

Printed in the U.S.A.
First Scholastic printing, March 2005

TABLE OF CONTENTS

Get Ready for a
FUN-WITH-FRIENDS ADVENTURE!

Hi, it's me, Strawberry Shortcake! Welcome back to Strawberryland! The door to my strawberry cottage is always open for a friend like you!

In this book, you'll find some of my favorite things to do when a friend comes to visit. We'll make crafts, share snacks, and play fun games together. And since friends share berry sweet memories, we'll also make a **memory book**!

I hope you'll like sharing the fun with one of your friends too! If you're ready, grab your **Friendship Craft Kit** and let's start our adventure!

Strawberry Shortcake's Tips for Getting Started

1. **Cover your work space with newspaper to keep it clean and neat.**

2. **It's a berry good idea to gather everything you need before starting a craft or recipe.**

3. **Whenever you see this picture throughout the book, it means that you can find what you need in your craft kit.**

4. **A lot of the materials that you'll need can be found around your house. You can get other supplies at a grocery or craft store.**

5. **You may need an adult's help with some activities in the book. Whenever you see this symbol, you'll know to ask for help.**

Berry Funny

Q: What does a flower call her best friend?

A: A bud!

Getting Ready to Decorate Your Memory Book

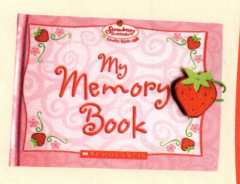

1. To open your memory book, stretch the elastic around the strawberry clasp so that you can slip it off. To close your memory book, stretch the elastic loop so you can slip it around the strawberry clasp again.

2. Write your name in the blank space on the first page of your memory book so that everyone will know it belongs to you.

3. Use a glue stick to attach paper scraps and photos to the pages of your memory book. Rub the glue all over the back of a piece of paper or photo, and press it onto the page. Smooth your fingers over the paper or photo to make it stick.

4. Some pages in your memory book have frames for pictures. Use scissors to trim your photos so they fit inside the frames.

5. Use white glue or craft glue to attach small treasures, like lace or pressed flowers, inside your memory book. Put small dots of glue on the back of each treasure and press it onto the page.

6. After you finish decorating a memory book page, let the page dry before closing the book.

Turn the page to make a memory book to hold all your berry special memories!

Friends Forever

Ask a friend to lend you a hand when you make this memory book page!

What You Need

- 🍓 Glitter pens
- 🍓 Construction paper
- 🍓 Scissors
- 🍓 Glue stick
- 🍓 Memory book

1. Use a glitter pen to trace around your friend's hand and fingers on a piece of construction paper. Then have your friend trace your hand on another sheet of paper.

2. Use your glitter pens to decorate each hand. Draw fingernails at the tip of every finger and add pretty rings. Color the fingernails different colors.

5. Write the word **FRIENDS** on one strip with a glitter pen. On the other strip, write **FOREVER**. Glue the strips across the wrists of the hands so they look like bracelets!

3. Use scissors to cut out each hand. Glue the hands onto a page of your memory book so the fingers overlap.

4. Tear two short, rectangular strips from construction paper. Each strip should be a little wider than each hand's wrist.

Here's More: Collect handprints from all of your friends! Write each friend's name on the wrist of the print. Write a word that describes the friend on each of the five fingers. Glue the hands onto the pages of your memory book.

Turn the page for a cute way to keep some memories in your back pocket!

- Pencil
- Ruler
- Construction paper
- Scissors
- Glitter pens
- Lace ribbon
- White glue or craft glue
- Glue stick
- Memory book
- Small treasures

Pockets Full of Memories

You can tuck tiny treasures into these berry cute paper pockets!

2. Decorate your pockets! Use a glitter pen to draw a dashed line for pretend stitching. Or add pretty swirls, flowers, or strawberries. It's up to you.

1. Measure and cut two 3-x-3$\frac{1}{2}$-inch rectangles out of construction paper. Snip two corners off one edge of both rectangles to make them look like pockets.

3. Place the lace ribbon on the top edge of a pocket. Cut off any extra lace. Use white glue to stick the lace to your pocket. Repeat on the other pocket.

4. Turn over the pocket so the decorated side is face down. Rub a glue stick along the sides and the bottom of the pocket (but not along the top edge).

5. Press each pocket to a page of your memory book so that three sides of the pocket stick to the paper. Repeat steps 4 and 5 with the second pocket.

6. Write POCKETS FULL OF MEMORIES on a sheet of paper with your glitter pens. Leave some extra space between each word. Cut the words out and glue them to your memory book pages.

7. Put photos, folded notes, tickets, trading cards, or other treasures from fun times with your friend in the pockets. Glue some extra treasures on the page for decoration, if you like.

Here's More: What else can you put in your pockets? Look around your house and see what you can find!

Turn the page for a sweet idea for remembering what you like best about a friend!

9

Berry Best Friends

What makes your berry best friend special? Make this memory book page to show how berry special your friendship is!

1. **Turn to a page in your memory book where you have two photo frames. Lay a thin white sheet of paper over one frame and trace the border of the frame. Cut the shape out. This will be your stencil.**

2. **Lay the paper shape over your photo or drawing. Trace around the shape on your photo, and cut your photo out. Repeat steps 1 and 2 on the other memory book frame and your other photo.**

What You Need

- Memory book
- 1 sheet of thin white paper
- Pencil
- Scissors
- Photos or drawings of yourself and a friend
- Glue stick
- Construction paper
- Foam stickers

3. Glue your photos onto the frames with a glue stick.

6. Write HERE'S WHAT I LIKE BEST ABOUT YOU on both hearts. Write your favorite things about your friend on one heart. Have your friend write her favorite things about you on the other heart. Glue both the hearts beside the photos.

4. Fold a 2-x-2-inch square of colored paper in half. Use a pencil to draw half a heart shape near the fold, as shown.

7. Peel off the paper backing from your foam stickers. Attach them all around the pages of your memory book for a berry cute decoration!

5. Carefully tear the folded paper along the line you drew in step 4. Unfold the paper to see a heart. Repeat steps 4 and 5 to make another heart.

Turn the page for flowers and leaves you can keep in your memory book!

Strawberry Shortcake's Pressed Flowers and Leaves

Pressed flowers and leaves can last forever on your memory book pages!

What You Need

- Fresh flowers and leaves
- Paper towels
- Scissors
- White paper
- Heavy books (like an old phone book or dictionary)
- White glue or craft glue

1. Take a walk outside and pick healthy flowers or fallen leaves from your yard or neighborhood. Thin flowers and leaves like pansies or clover are best.

2. Once you've collected your flowers and leaves, take them inside and lay them out to dry on paper towels (if they are wet). If there are any stems, trim them so they are about two inches long.

3. Open a heavy book (like an old phone book) to the middle. Place one sheet of white paper on top of a page.

4. Arrange your flowers and leaves on the paper, with space between them. Put your flowers face down (if you can) so they'll be easier to press.

6. Let your flowers and leaves dry for about two weeks, then check on them. If they are still a little damp, leave them in the book for another week. If they are dry and feel like paper, they are done!

5. Lay a second sheet of white paper on top of the flowers and leaves. Carefully close the book so that the flowers and leaves are in between the two sheets of paper. Stack more books on top to make the pressing go faster.

7. Use white glue to attach your pressed flowers and leaves to pages in your memory book!

Turn the page to see how to keep a whole year of berry good memories!

Four Seasons of Fun

Winter, spring, summer, and fall—
sweet friends are the best of all!

14

What You Need

- Scissors
- Pencil
- Ruler
- Construction paper
- Glue stick
- Memory book
- Glitter pens
- White glue or craft glue
- Found treasures
  (like leaves, flowers,
  tags, buttons, gems,
  and photos)

1. Cut out four 2-x-3-inch rectangles from different sheets of colored construction paper. Use a glue stick to attach the rectangles onto two pages in your memory book, as shown.

2. Cut four 1-x-2-inch rectangles from construction paper. Snip two corners from one short side of the rectangle to make a tag. Repeat on all the rectangles.

3. Use your glitter pens to write WINTER, SPRING, SUMMER, and FALL on the tags. One season should go on each tag. Glue one tag on each rectangle on your memory book pages. Let dry.

Here are some treasure ideas:

For **winter**, you might collect a little yarn from your scarf, fold and cut paper snowflakes, or save a piece of gift wrap from a holiday gift.

For **spring**, find a new leaf or bud to glue onto the page. Draw a picture of the first butterfly you see.

For **summer**, glue on bright pressed flowers or watermelon seeds from a picnic lunch.

For **fall**, collect brightly colored leaves, feathers, and seeds from apples and pumpkins, and glue them onto your pages.

4. Collect and make little treasures to glue onto each season in your memory book.

Turn the page to see your friends flutter, float, and fly!

Fluttery Friends

What's even better than butterflies?
Berry friendly butterflies!

What You Need

- 🍓 Memory book
- 🍓 Glitter pens
- 🍓 Construction paper
- 🍓 Scissors
- 🍓 Glue stick
- 🍓 Photos of yourself and your friends (optional)

1. **Make butterflies! Fold a 3-x-3-inch piece of paper in half. Use scissors to cut two big humps along the open edges, so the paper looks like the letter B. Open the paper to see your butterfly. Make three more butterflies.**

2. **Color in the body of each butterfly and decorate its wings. Will you draw stripes or spots or other designs? It's up to you!**

5. Write the words MY FRIENDS AND ME in fancy letters with glitter pens on colored paper. Leave some space between each word. Cut the words out.

3. Cut out a friend's face from a photo, or draw her picture and cut it out. Glue the face to a butterfly. With a glitter pen, write your friend's name on the butterfly's body.

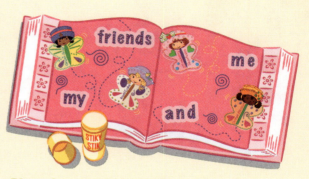

6. Glue the words onto your memory book page. Place them around the butterflies, any way you like. Decorate the page with your glitter pens.

4. Rub glue on the fold of one butterfly. Press the glued part onto one of your memory book pages. Glue all your butterflies onto two pages of your memory book.

Turn the page for an activity that will make you smile!

My Memory Book: Miles of Smiles

Gather some smiles for a page that reminds you of what makes you berry happy!

1. **Look through the pages of some old magazines or catalogs. Cut out the smiles from the pictures. You'll need about 10 smiles.**

2. **With your glitter pens, write SMILE! in fancy letters on a sheet of construction paper. Leave spaces between each letter. Cut the letters out and decorate the squares with glitter pens.**

5. Arrange all 10 of your smiles on two pages. Glue the smiles in place with a glue stick.

3. Glue the letters across the top of two memory book pages with a glue stick.

6. What makes you smile? Write words and draw pictures around the page of things that make you smile!

4. Glue your smile cut-outs to a sheet of construction paper. Cut around each of these smiles to make a colored border.

Turn the page to play Strawberry Shortcake's button matching game!

19

Hide and Seek Button Game

Can you find the ten pairs of matching buttons on these two pages?
Look berry carefully!

Turn the page to take a peek in
Strawberry Shortcake's memory book!

Strawberry Shortcake's Memory Book Game

Take a close look at these objects and pictures from my memory book. Each object is from a different fun time with one of my friends—Angel Cake, Orange Blossom, Ginger Snap, Blueberry Muffin—or my little sister, Apple Dumplin.
Can you match each object with the correct picture of my fun memory?

A.

B.

C.

D.

E.

F.

1.

2.

3.

5.

4.

6.

See page 38 for the answers.

Turn the page to invite a friend to play!

23

Strawberry Shortcake's Berry Happy Invitation

Since my friends live in nearby lands like Cakewalk and Cookie Corners, sometimes I send them a berry special invitation to come visit! You can make an invitation too!

What You Need

- 🍓 Pencil
- 🍓 Ruler
- 🍓 Construction paper or card stock (yellow and pink)
- 🍓 Scissors
- 🍓 Ribbon
- 🍓 School glue or glue stick
- 🍓 Glitter pens
- 🍓 Optional: Envelope

1. Use a ruler and pencil to measure a 5-x-6-inch rectangle on a sheet of yellow construction paper or card stock. Cut it out.

2. Glue a 7-inch piece of ribbon onto the middle of the yellow rectangle so the ends stick out from the sides.

3. Now cut a 4-x-5-inch rectangle from the pink construction paper or card stock. Use glitter pens to decorate the edges of the paper. What will you draw? Strawberries, flowers, or maybe swirls? It's up to you!

6. Your invitation is ready! You can deliver your note in person or put it in an envelope and mail it.

4. Measure and cut another rectangle—this time 3-x-4 inches—from yellow paper. Use a glitter pen to write your invitation message. Make sure to include the day and time you want your friend to come over.

Here's More: To mail your invitation, write your friend's address neatly on the front of the envelope. Write your address in the top left corner and place a stamp in the top right corner. Then put the invitation in the mailbox!

Srawberry Shortcake
Strawberryland

Ginger Snap
Cookie Corners

5. Glue the pink rectangle onto the yellow rectangle that has the ribbon. Glue the smaller yellow rectangle on top.

Turn the page to make a friendship gift that's right on the button!

Berry Best Friend Button Bracelet

Every friendship is special! Make a button bracelet to give to your berry best pal.

What You Need

- Waxed paper or aluminum foil
- Buttons
- Lace ribbon
- White glue or craft glue
- Scissors

1. Lay a sheet of waxed paper or aluminum foil on a flat table.

2. Place seven buttons, in any order that you like, in a row on your wax paper or aluminum foil. The buttons should be face down so that the backs are showing.

3. Put a drop of white glue in the center of each button.

4. Cut a piece of lace ribbon that's 10 inches long. Place the lace over the buttons so that the buttons are in the middle of the lace, as shown.

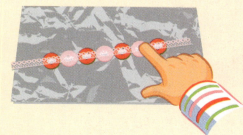

5. Use your finger to press the lace into the glue. Let dry.

6. Take your bracelet off the waxed paper or aluminum foil and turn it over, so that the buttons are on top. Pick off any dried glue on the front of the buttons. Tie the ends of the bracelet around your friend's wrist.

Here's More: Make one bracelet for yourself and one bracelet for your berry best friend!

Turn the page to make a craft that lets your fingers play!

Strawberry Shortcake's Finger Puppet Friends

Say hello with these finger puppet friends!

What You Need

* A pair of gloves (each friend uses one glove)
* 5 tissues
* Ribbon, yarn, or thread
* Markers
* Scissors
* White glue or craft glue
* Craft scraps (like paper, fabric, old buttons, sequins, or beads)

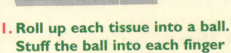

Tissues

1. Roll up each tissue into a ball. Stuff the ball into each finger of a glove.

2. Tie a piece of ribbon or yarn around the outside of the glove, just below each tissue ball to make your finger puppet heads.

3. Draw a face on each head with a marker. Glue on sequins or beads for eyes, if you like.

4. Add hair by gluing yarn, twine, or pieces of paper on each head.

6. Put your hand inside the glove. Wiggle your fingers. Tell riddles or sing songs with your finger puppet friends!

5. Use yarn, fabric scraps, or paper to dress each of your finger puppet friends. Cut a T-shape to make a shirt. Cut a V-shape to make pants. Cut a triangle to make a dress. Glue the scraps onto each finger puppet and let dry.

Turn the page to make some berry special blooms!

29

Strawberry Shortcake's Berry Beautiful Blossoms

Make strings of colorful paper flowers with a friend!

1. Cut four strips of construction paper that are 8 inches long and as wide as your thumb (about $\frac{1}{2}$ inch wide). All four strips can be the same color or different colors.

What You Need

- Construction paper
- Scissors
- Glue
- Pencil
- String, yarn, or ribbon
- Tape

2. Glue two paper strips together to make an **X**, as shown.

3. Glue the other two paper strips across the **X** to make a star.

4. Cut a small circle from construction paper. Glue it in the middle of the star for a flower center. Let dry.

5. Snip each strip down the middle so each one looks like it's two strips. Roll each strip around a pencil to make it curly.

6. Cut a short piece of string, ribbon, or yarn (about 12 inches long). Tape your flower to each end of the string. Make more **Berry Beautiful Blossoms** and hang them up anywhere you like!

Here's More:

🍓 Make lots of blossoms and tape them all to one long string to hang as a chain!

🍓 Attach single flowers to packages or cards for decorations.

🍓 Tie short strings to the handlebars of your bikes when you and a friend go bike riding together!

Turn the page to make a cute carry-all to hold special treasures!

Strawberry Shortcake's Craft Carry-All

$\mathbb{M}$ake your own carry-all
to hold the treasures
you make and find with a friend!

What You Need

- Colored paper, gift wrap, or old magazines
- Scissors
- White glue or craft glue
- Empty cereal box
- Ribbon or yarn
- Tape (optional)

1. Cut colored paper, gift wrap, or old magazine pages into squares the size of the palm of your hand.

2. Use your finger to spread glue on the back of a paper square. Press the square onto the cereal box. Glue more paper squares onto the cereal box until it's completely covered.

3. Cut out two big heart shapes from colored paper, gift wrap, or old magazine pages. Glue one heart to each side of the box.

4. Ask a grown-up to help you poke a hole on the sides of the box with scissors, as shown.

5. Cut a piece of ribbon or yarn about two feet long. Poke each end of the ribbon or yarn through one hole on the sides of the box. Glue or tape the ends inside the box to make a handle for your carry-all.

6. Use your carry-all to store crafts and other special stuff you and a friend make or find together.

Here's More: Here's what you might put inside your carry-all after a day with a friend!

🍓 A flower you find on a walk

🍓 A bag of cookies you bake together

🍓 A picture your friend gives to you

Turn the page for sweet snacks to share!

Crunchy Crunch Mix

This crispy combination is berry nice to share with a friend!

1. **Pour the cereal, pretzel twists, and peanuts into a large bowl.**

2. **Mix everything together with a wooden spoon.**

What You Need

- 🍓 1 cup of dry cereal (any kind)
- 🍓 1 cup of mini-pretzel twists
- 🍓 ½ cup honey-roasted or regular peanuts
- 🍓 Utensils: Large bowl, measuring cups, wooden spoon

Serves: 2 berry best friends

3. **Crunch and munch together!**

Turn the page for a sweet strawberry snack!

Strawberry Jam Sandwiches

This sweet strawberry snack is straight from the heart!

What You Need

- Pencil
- Paper
- Scissors
- 3 slices of bread
- 2 teaspoons of strawberry jam
- Utensils: butter knife, measuring spoon

Makes: 1 berry sweet sandwich

1. Draw a heart shape on a piece of paper. Cut out the heart and put it on top of a slice of bread. Carefully cut around the pattern with a butter knife.

2. Pull away the extra bread to leave a heart shape. Repeat with the other two slices of bread, so you have three hearts all together.

3. Spread 1 teaspoon of jam on top of the first heart. Place the second heart on top of the jam.

4. Spread 1 teaspoon of jam on top of the second heart. Place the third heart on top.

Turn the page to dip into a yummy snack with a friend!

Delish Dip and Veggies

Colorful veggies around a bowl of creamy dip look so berry pretty on the snack table!

What You Need

- 1 (8-ounce) container of sour cream (about 1 cup)
- 1 (8-ounce) container of plain yogurt (about ¾ cup)
- 0.4 ounce envelope of dry salad dressing mix (about 1 tablespoon)
- Your favorite vegetables (like carrots, celery, broccoli, cherry tomatoes, or peppers)
- Paper towels
- Utensils: Medium mixing bowl, wooden spoon, large plate

Makes: About 2 cups of dip

1. Spoon the sour cream and yogurt into the bowl.

2. Add the dry salad dressing mix. Stir everything together with the wooden spoon.

3. Put the bowl of dip in the middle of a big plate.

6. Place the veggies all around the plate. Dunk a veggie into the dip and eat!

4. What kinds of veggies would you like to have with your dip? Gather them together. Wash them in cold water and dry them with paper towels.

What are your favorite veggies?

- carrot sticks?
- green or yellow pepper strips?
- broccoli flowerets?
- cherry tomatoes?
- cucumber rounds?
- sugar snap peas?
- celery sticks?

5. Let a grown-up help you cut or break the veggies into bite-sized pieces.

Here's More: Try your dip with pretzels, crackers, or breadsticks! It's yummylicious!

Strawberry Shortcake's Answer Page

Hide and Seek Button Game (pages 20-21)

Strawberry Shortcake's Memory Book Game

(pages 22-23)

1 – F
2 – B
3 – C
4 – A
5 – D
6 – E